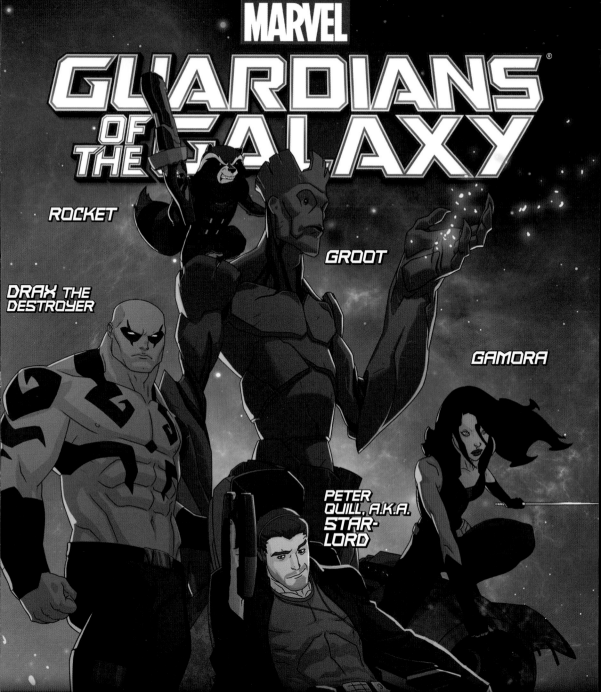

MARVEL
GUARDIANS OF THE GALAXY

ROCKET

GROOT

DRAX THE DESTROYER

GAMORA

PETER QUILL, A.K.A. STAR-LORD

PREVIOUSLY:
The Guardians came into possession of a mysterious Spartaxan cube that holds a map to an object of immense power called the Cosmic Seed. Half Spartaxan, Star-Lord is the only one able to access the map. Now the Guardians must find the Seed before Thanos does.

Volume 8: Hitchin' A Ride
BASED ON THE DISNEY XD ANIMATED TV SERIES

Written by DAVID McDERMOTT   Directed by JEFF WAMESTER
Animation Art Produced by MARVEL ANIMATION STUDIOS   Adapted by JOE CARAMAGNA

Special Thanks to
HANNAH MACDONALD & PRODUCT FACTORY and ANTHONY GAMBINO

MARK BASSO editor
AXEL ALONSO editor in chief
DAN BUCKLEY publisher

MARK PANICCIA senior editor
JOE QUESADA chief creative officer
ALAN FINE executive producer

ABDOBOOKS.COM

Reinforced library bound edition published in 2020 by Spotlight,
a division of ABDO, PO Box 398166, Minneapolis, Minnesota 55439.
Spotlight produces high-quality reinforced library bound editions for
schools and libraries. Published by agreement with Marvel Characters, Inc.

Printed in the United States of America, North Mankato, Minnesota.
042019
092019

THIS BOOK CONTAINS
RECYCLED MATERIALS

marvelkids.com
© 2020 MARVEL

Library of Congress Control Number: 2018965974

Publisher's Cataloging-in-Publication Data

Names: Caramagna, Joe; McDermott, David, authors. | Marvel Animation Studios,
    illustrator.
Title: Hitchin' a ride / by Joe Caramagna ; David McDermott; illustrated by Marvel
    Animation Studios.
Description: Minneapolis, Minnesota : Spotlight, 2020. | Series: Guardians of the
    Galaxy set 3 ; volume 8
Summary: Groot becomes infected by a super-evolved Symbiote and Rocket goes
    to great lengths to save him; Star-Lord protects the Cosmic Seed map when
    Yondu's Ravagers appear.
Identifiers: ISBN 9781532143595 (lib. bdg.)
Subjects: LCSH: Guardians of the Galaxy (Fictitious characters)--Juvenile fiction. |
    Superheroes--Juvenile fiction. | Space aliens--Juvenile fiction. | Infectious
    diseases--Juvenile fiction. | Graphic novels--Juvenile fiction. | Space--Juvenile
    fiction. | Comic books, strips, etc--Juvenile fiction.
Classification: DDC 741.5--dc23

Spotlight

A Division of ABDO
abdobooks.com

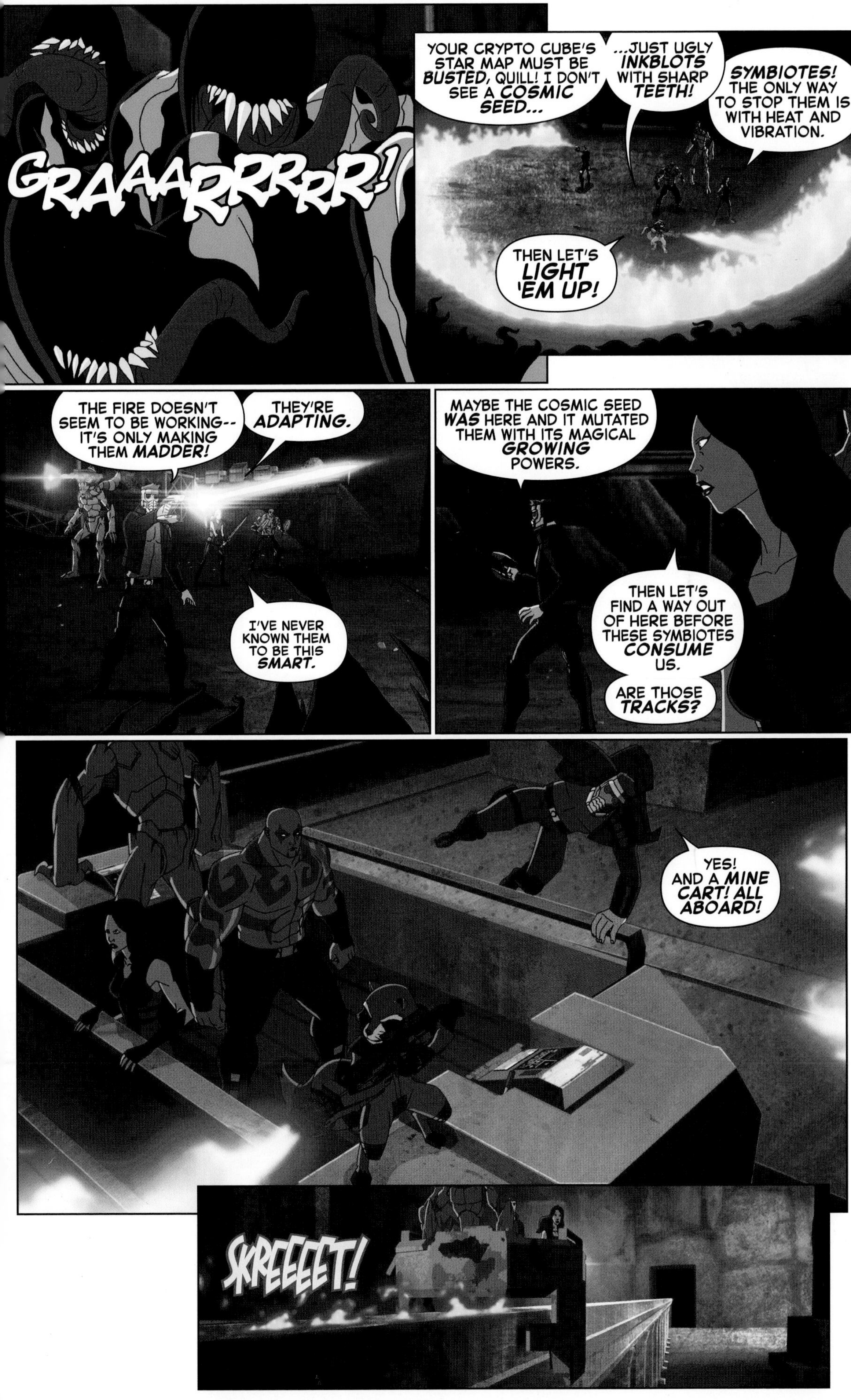
GRAAARRRRR!
YOUR CRYPTO CUBE'S STAR MAP MUST BE BUSTED, QUILL! I DON'T SEE A COSMIC SEED...
...JUST UGLY INKBLOTS WITH SHARP TEETH!
SYMBIOTES! THE ONLY WAY TO STOP THEM IS WITH HEAT AND VIBRATION.
THEN LET'S LIGHT 'EM UP!
THE FIRE DOESN'T SEEM TO BE WORKING-- IT'S ONLY MAKING THEM MADDER!
THEY'RE ADAPTING.
I'VE NEVER KNOWN THEM TO BE THIS SMART.
MAYBE THE COSMIC SEED WAS HERE AND IT MUTATED THEM WITH ITS MAGICAL GROWING POWERS.
THEN LET'S FIND A WAY OUT OF HERE BEFORE THESE SYMBIOTES CONSUME US.
ARE THOSE TRACKS?
YES! AND A MINE CART! ALL ABOARD!
SKREEEEET!

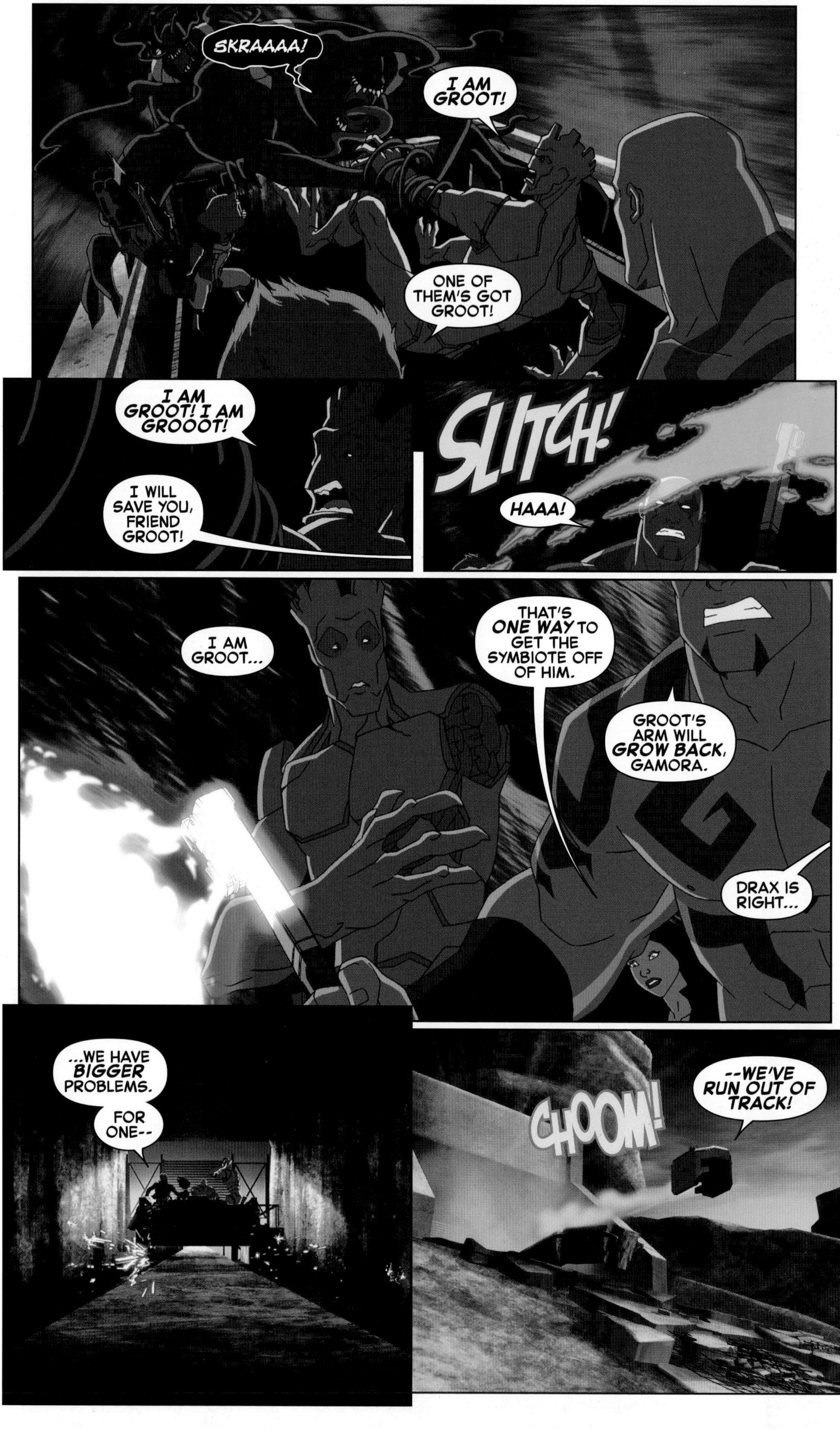
SKRAAAA!
I AM GROOT!
ONE OF THEM'S GOT GROOT!
I AM GROOT! I AM GROOOT!
I WILL SAVE YOU, FRIEND GROOT!
SLITCH!
HAAA!
I AM GROOT...
THAT'S ONE WAY TO GET THE SYMBIOTE OFF OF HIM.
GROOT'S ARM WILL GROW BACK, GAMORA.
DRAX IS RIGHT...
...WE HAVE BIGGER PROBLEMS.
FOR ONE--
CHOOM!
--WE'VE RUN OUT OF TRACK!

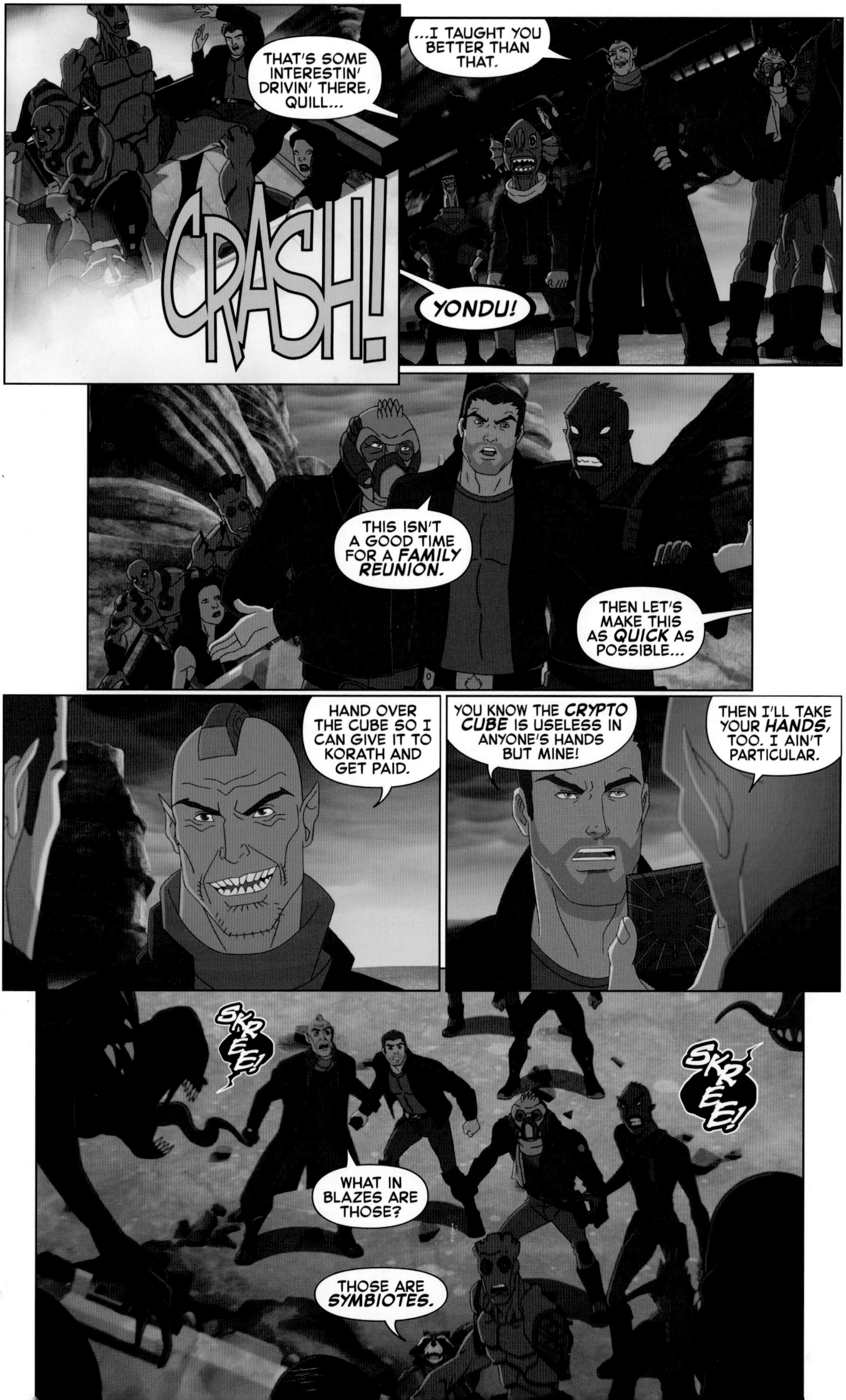

THAT'S SOME INTERESTIN' DRIVIN' THERE, QUILL...
CRASH!
...I TAUGHT YOU BETTER THAN THAT.
YONDU!
THIS ISN'T A GOOD TIME FOR A FAMILY REUNION.
THEN LET'S MAKE THIS AS QUICK AS POSSIBLE...
HAND OVER THE CUBE SO I CAN GIVE IT TO KORATH AND GET PAID.
YOU KNOW THE CRYPTO CUBE IS USELESS IN ANYONE'S HANDS BUT MINE!
THEN I'LL TAKE YOUR HANDS, TOO. I AIN'T PARTICULAR.
SKREE!
SKREE!
WHAT IN BLAZES ARE THOSE?
THOSE ARE SYMBIOTES.

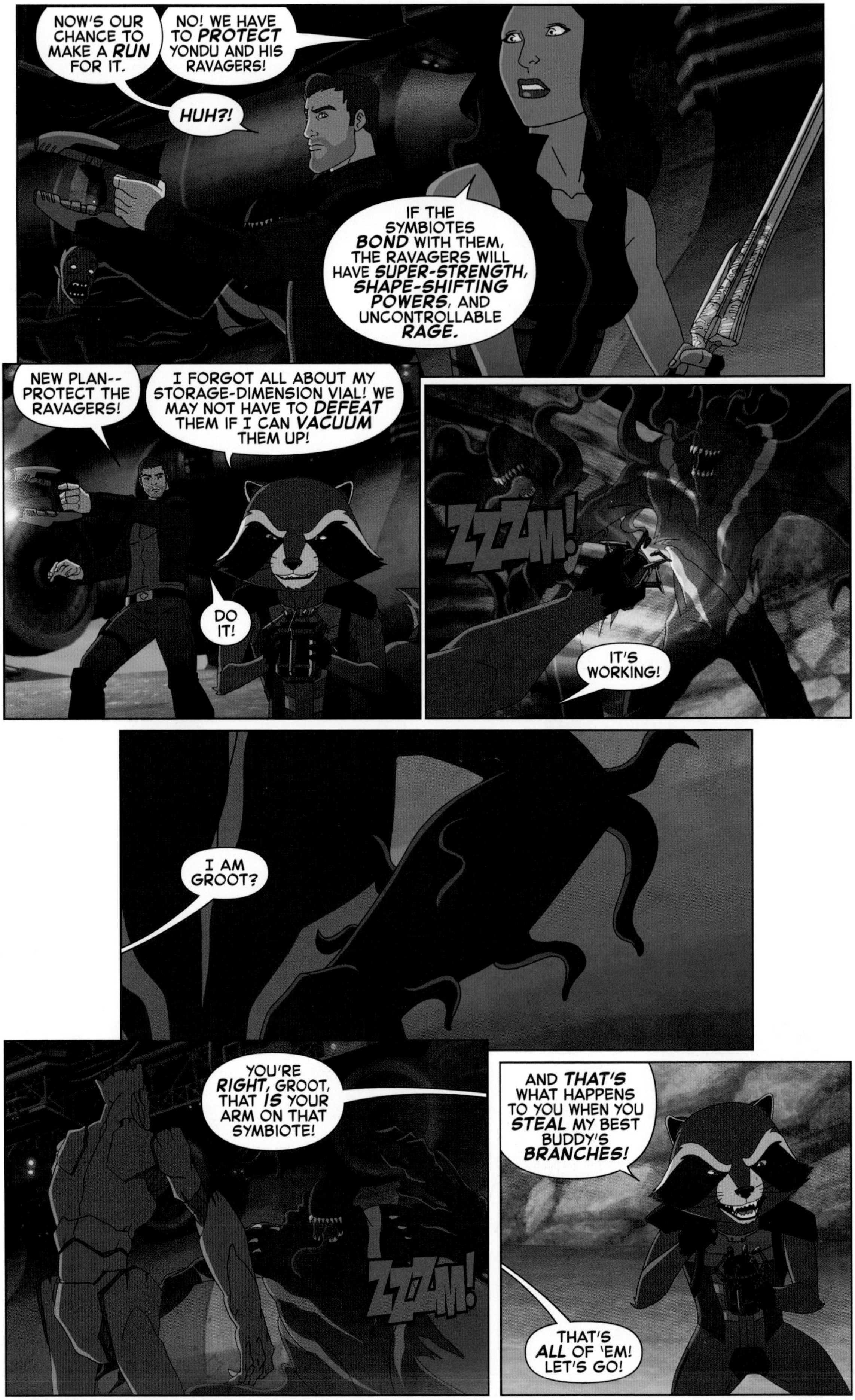
NOW'S OUR CHANCE TO MAKE A RUN FOR IT.
NO! WE HAVE TO PROTECT YONDU AND HIS RAVAGERS!
HUH?!
IF THE SYMBIOTES BOND WITH THEM, THE RAVAGERS WILL HAVE SUPER-STRENGTH, SHAPE-SHIFTING POWERS, AND UNCONTROLLABLE RAGE.
NEW PLAN-- PROTECT THE RAVAGERS!
I FORGOT ALL ABOUT MY STORAGE-DIMENSION VIAL! WE MAY NOT HAVE TO DEFEAT THEM IF I CAN VACUUM THEM UP!
DO IT!
ZZZAM!
IT'S WORKING!
I AM GROOT?
YOU'RE RIGHT, GROOT, THAT IS YOUR ARM ON THAT SYMBIOTE!
ZZZAM!
AND THAT'S WHAT HAPPENS TO YOU WHEN YOU STEAL MY BEST BUDDY'S BRANCHES!
THAT'S ALL OF 'EM! LET'S GO!

AND DON'T EVEN *THINK* ABOUT FOLLOWING US, YONDU, OR ROCKET'LL SUCK YOU UP INTO THE STORAGE DIMENSION, TOO!

OH, AND YONDU?

"GIVE MY BROTHER KORATH MY REGARDS."

MY CRYPTO CUBE LIT UP DOWN THERE, SO THE COSMIC SEED *WAS* THERE AT SOME POINT...

...UNLESS IT'S JUST *MESSING* WITH US. BUT AT LEAST WE GOT OFF THE PLANET OF THE SYMBIOTES UNHARMED.

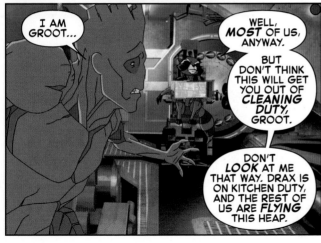

I AM GROOT...

WELL, *MOST* OF US, ANYWAY.

BUT DON'T THINK THIS WILL GET YOU OUT OF *CLEANING DUTY*, GROOT.

DON'T *LOOK* AT ME THAT WAY. DRAX IS ON KITCHEN DUTY, AND THE REST OF US ARE *FLYING* THIS HEAP.

I AM GROOT.

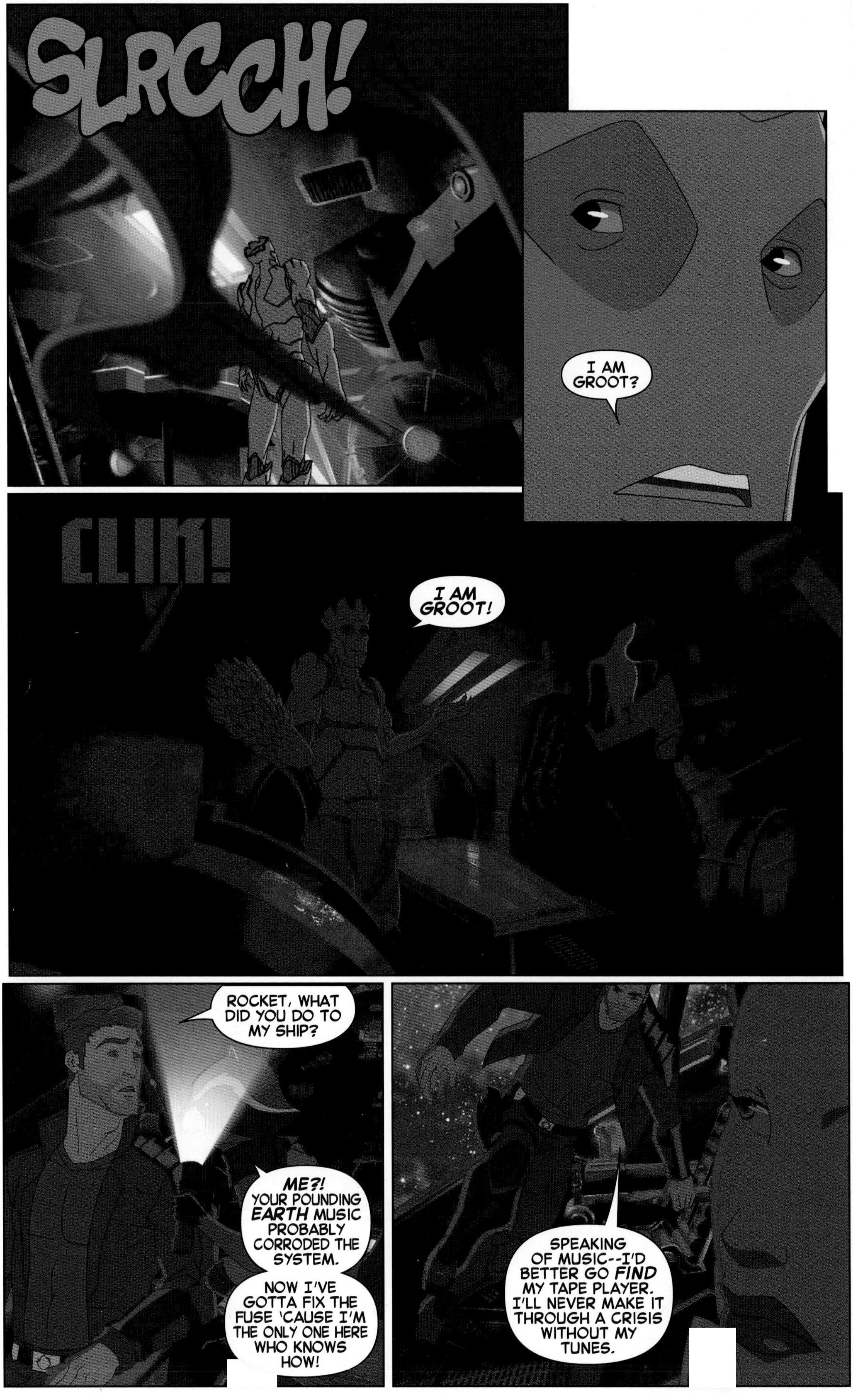
SLRCCH!
I AM GROOT?
CLIK!
I AM GROOT!
ROCKET, WHAT DID YOU DO TO MY SHIP?
ME?! YOUR POUNDING EARTH MUSIC PROBABLY CORRODED THE SYSTEM.
NOW I'VE GOTTA FIX THE FUSE 'CAUSE I'M THE ONLY ONE HERE WHO KNOWS HOW!
SPEAKING OF MUSIC--I'D BETTER GO FIND MY TAPE PLAYER. I'LL NEVER MAKE IT THROUGH A CRISIS WITHOUT MY TUNES.

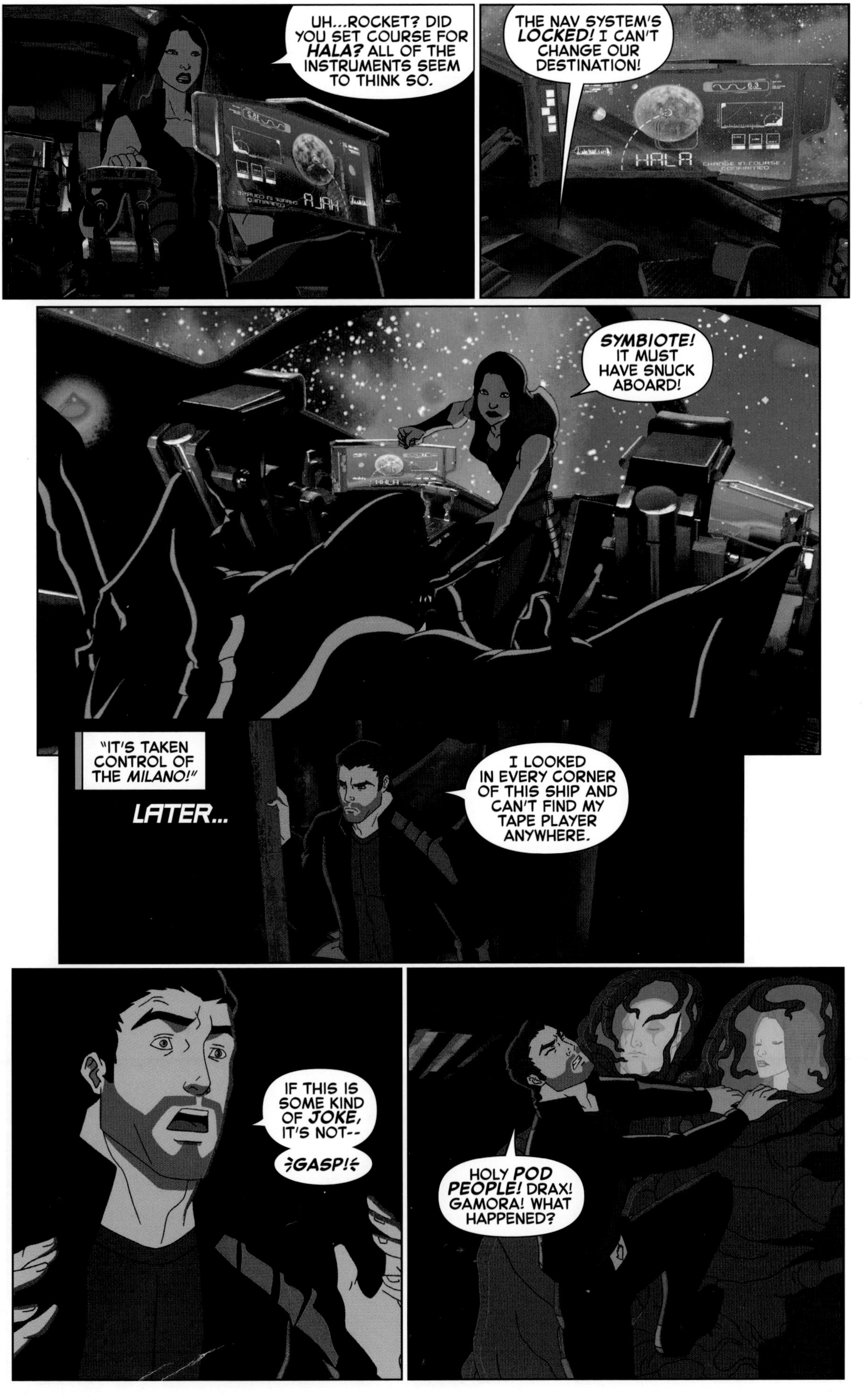

UH...ROCKET? DID YOU SET COURSE FOR *HALA?* ALL OF THE INSTRUMENTS SEEM TO THINK SO.
THE NAV SYSTEM'S *LOCKED!* I CAN'T CHANGE OUR DESTINATION!
HALA
SYMBIOTE! IT MUST HAVE SNUCK ABOARD!
"IT'S TAKEN CONTROL OF THE *MILANO!*"
LATER...
I LOOKED IN EVERY CORNER OF THIS SHIP AND CAN'T FIND MY TAPE PLAYER ANYWHERE.
IF THIS IS SOME KIND OF *JOKE,* IT'S NOT--
GASP!
HOLY *POD PEOPLE!* DRAX! GAMORA! WHAT HAPPENED?

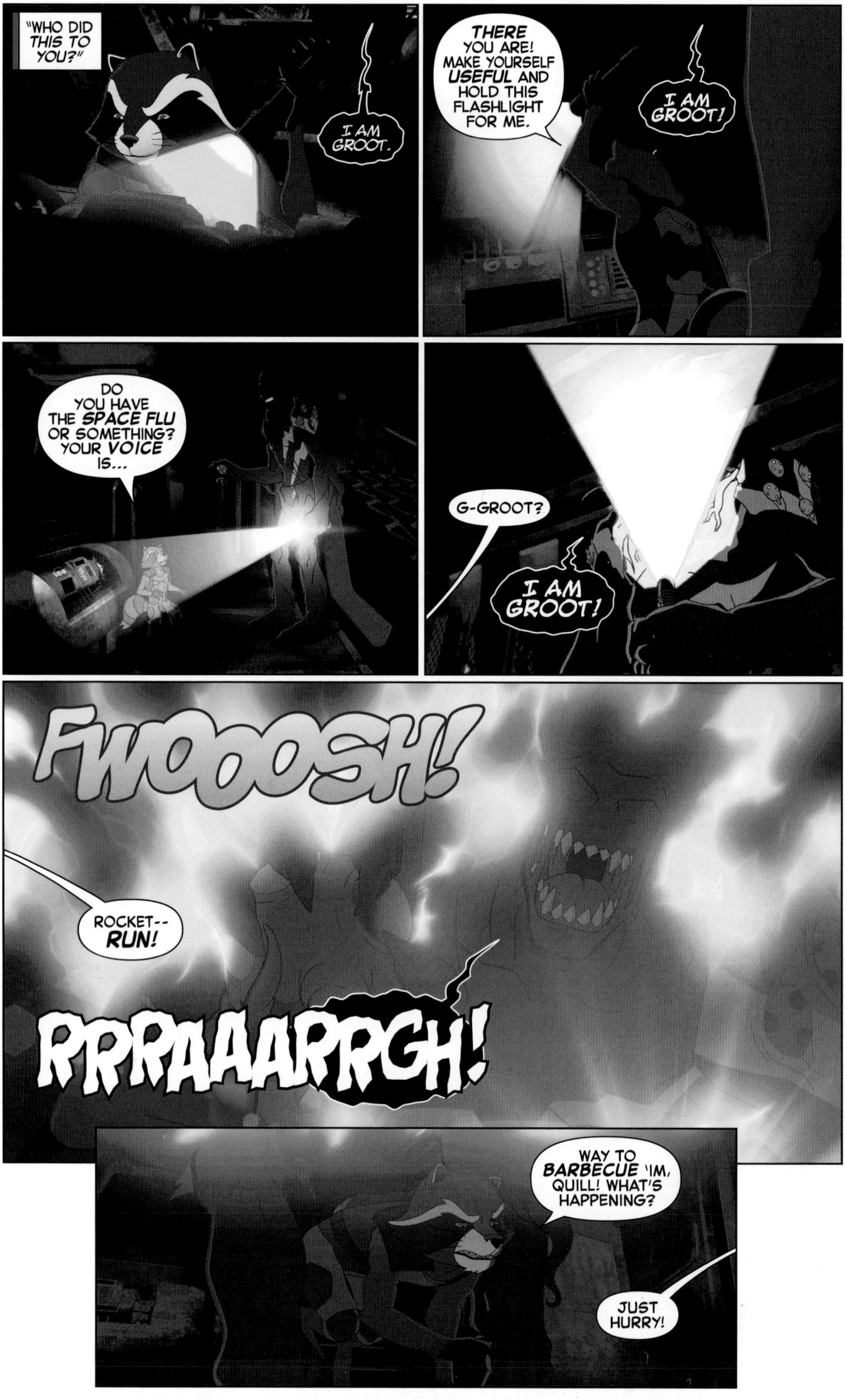
"WHO DID THIS TO YOU?"
I AM GROOT.
THERE YOU ARE! MAKE YOURSELF USEFUL AND HOLD THIS FLASHLIGHT FOR ME.
I AM GROOT!
DO YOU HAVE THE SPACE FLU OR SOMETHING? YOUR VOICE IS...
G-GROOT?
I AM GROOT!
FWOOOSH!
ROCKET-- RUN!
RRRAAARRGH!
WAY TO BARBECUE 'IM, QUILL! WHAT'S HAPPENING?
JUST HURRY!

A *SYMBIOTE* TOOK CONTROL OF THE SHIP! IT TRAPPED DRAX AND GAMORA! AND NOW IT LOOKS LIKE IT HAS GROOT!

WHAT DO WE DO?

OUR *TRADITIONAL* WEAPONS WON'T WORK ON IT, I'LL HAVE TO BUILD US A *NEW* ONE.

BUT I NEED *TIME.*

FUSING THE DOOR SHUT SHOULD KEEP IT OUT OF HERE FOR A WHILE.

FsSSs!

SURE, THEY HATE FIRE, BUT THE WAY TO DEFEAT THEM IS WITH *VIBRATIONS.*

THE KIND WE GET FROM YOUR EARTH RACKET.

YOU HAD MY TAPE PLAYER?

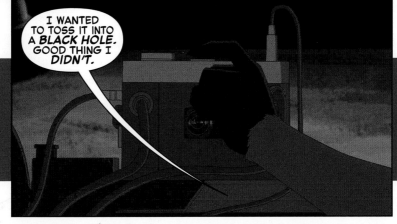

I WANTED TO TOSS IT INTO A *BLACK HOLE.* GOOD THING I *DIDN'T.*

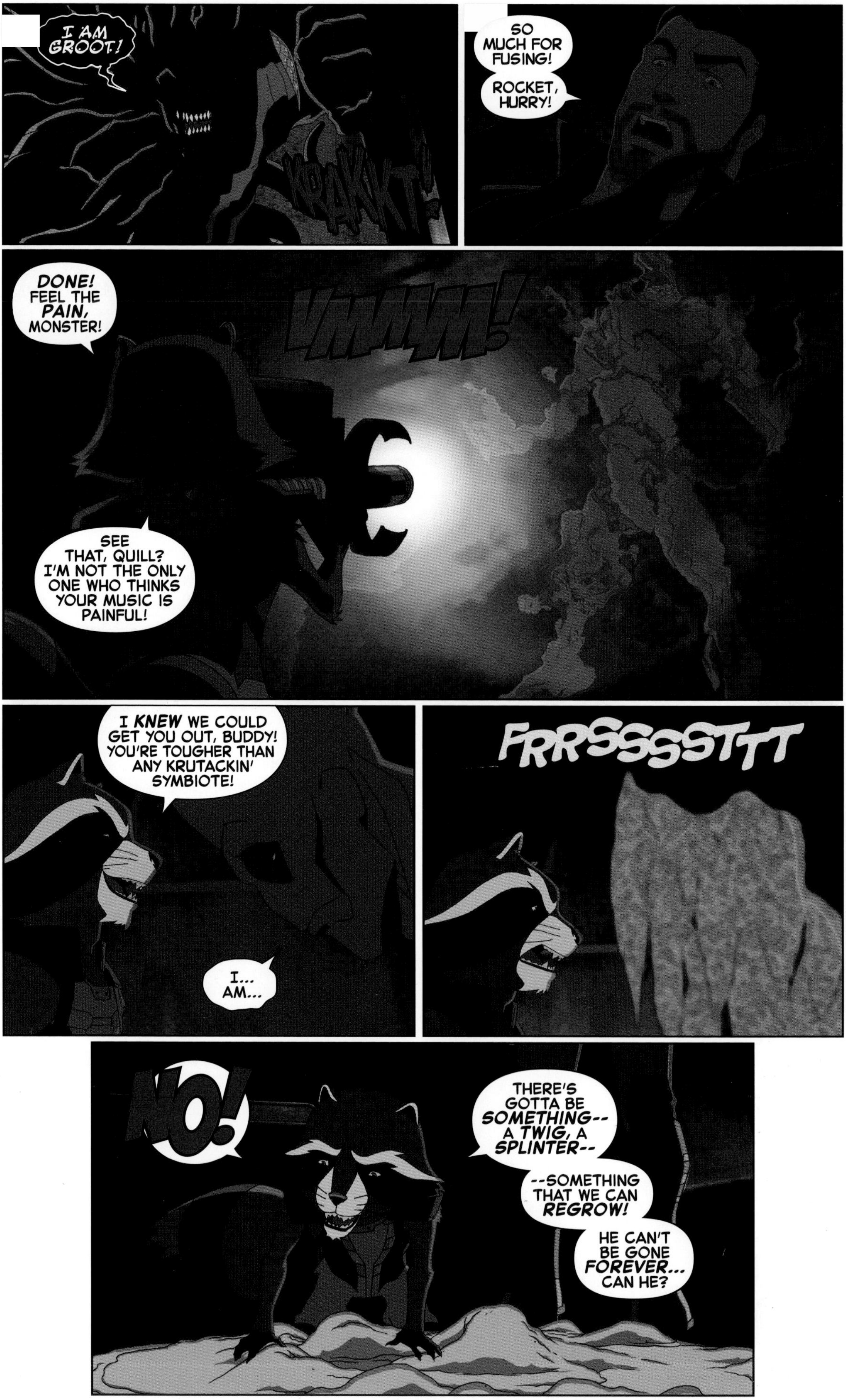
I AM GROOT!
KRAKKT!
SO MUCH FOR FUSING!
ROCKET, HURRY!
DONE! FEEL THE PAIN, MONSTER!
VMMMM!
SEE THAT, QUILL? I'M NOT THE ONLY ONE WHO THINKS YOUR MUSIC IS PAINFUL!
I KNEW WE COULD GET YOU OUT, BUDDY! YOU'RE TOUGHER THAN ANY KRUTACKIN' SYMBIOTE!
I... AM...
FRRSSSSSTTT
NO!
THERE'S GOTTA BE SOMETHING-- A TWIG, A SPLINTER--
--SOMETHING THAT WE CAN REGROW!
HE CAN'T BE GONE FOREVER... CAN HE?

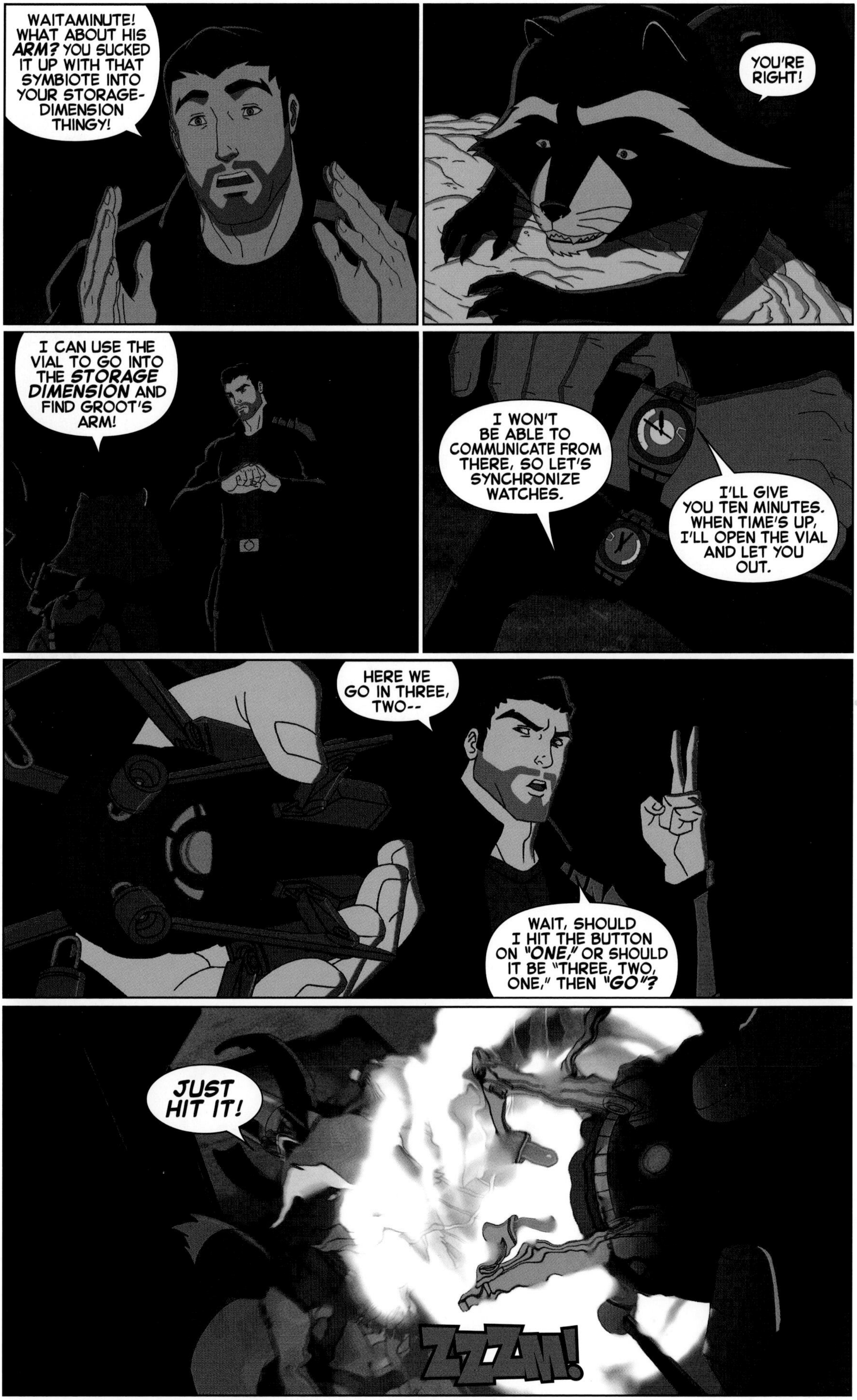
WAITAMINUTE! WHAT ABOUT HIS ARM? YOU SUCKED IT UP WITH THAT SYMBIOTE INTO YOUR STORAGE-DIMENSION THINGY!
YOU'RE RIGHT!
I CAN USE THE VIAL TO GO INTO THE STORAGE DIMENSION AND FIND GROOT'S ARM!
I WON'T BE ABLE TO COMMUNICATE FROM THERE, SO LET'S SYNCHRONIZE WATCHES.
I'LL GIVE YOU TEN MINUTES. WHEN TIME'S UP, I'LL OPEN THE VIAL AND LET YOU OUT.
HERE WE GO IN THREE, TWO--
WAIT, SHOULD I HIT THE BUTTON ON "ONE," OR SHOULD IT BE "THREE, TWO, ONE," THEN "GO"?
JUST HIT IT!
ZZZAM!

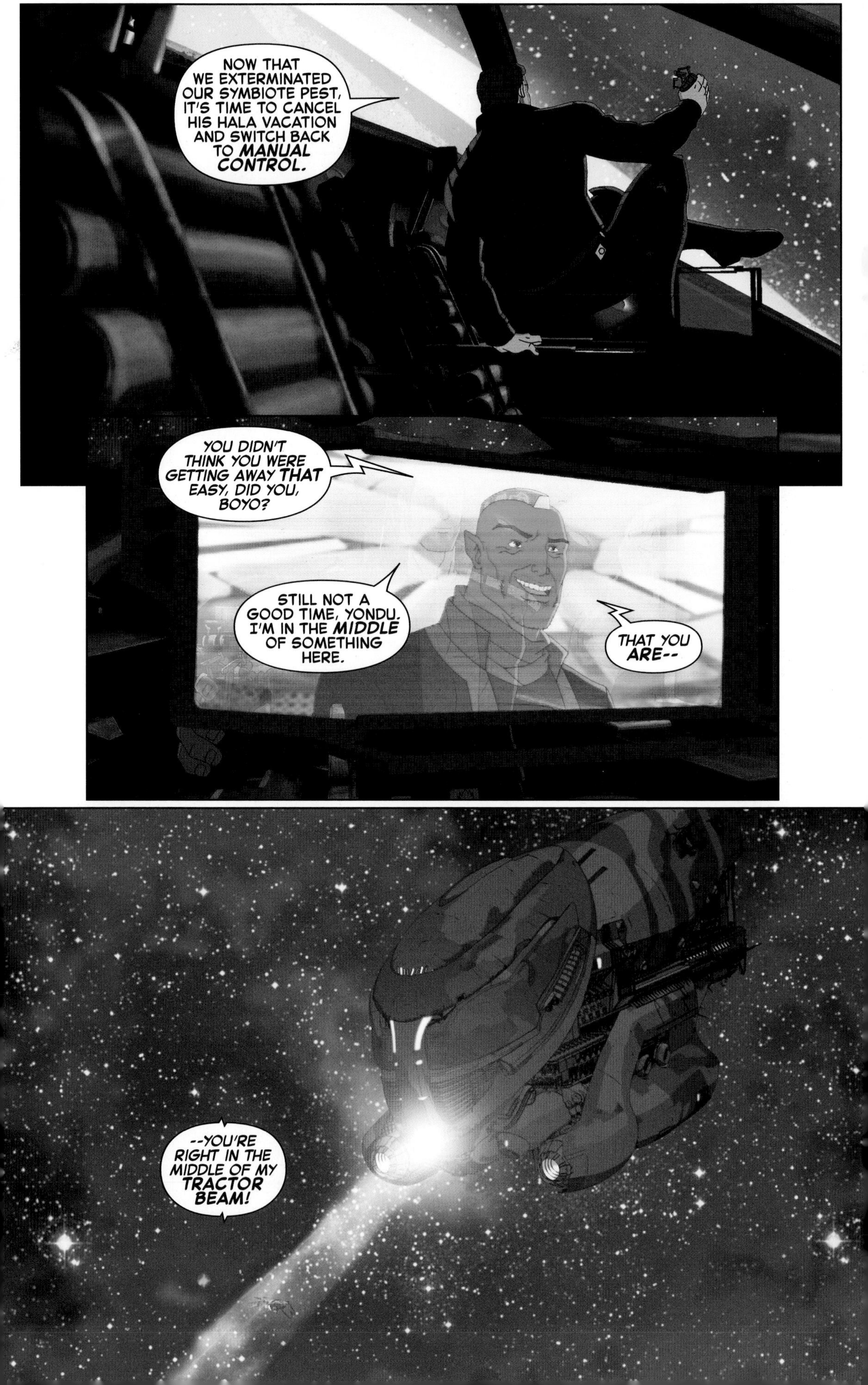
NOW THAT WE EXTERMINATED OUR SYMBIOTE PEST, IT'S TIME TO CANCEL HIS HALA VACATION AND SWITCH BACK TO MANUAL CONTROL.
YOU DIDN'T THINK YOU WERE GETTING AWAY THAT EASY, DID YOU, BOYO?
STILL NOT A GOOD TIME, YONDU. I'M IN THE MIDDLE OF SOMETHING HERE.
THAT YOU ARE--
--YOU'RE RIGHT IN THE MIDDLE OF MY TRACTOR BEAM!

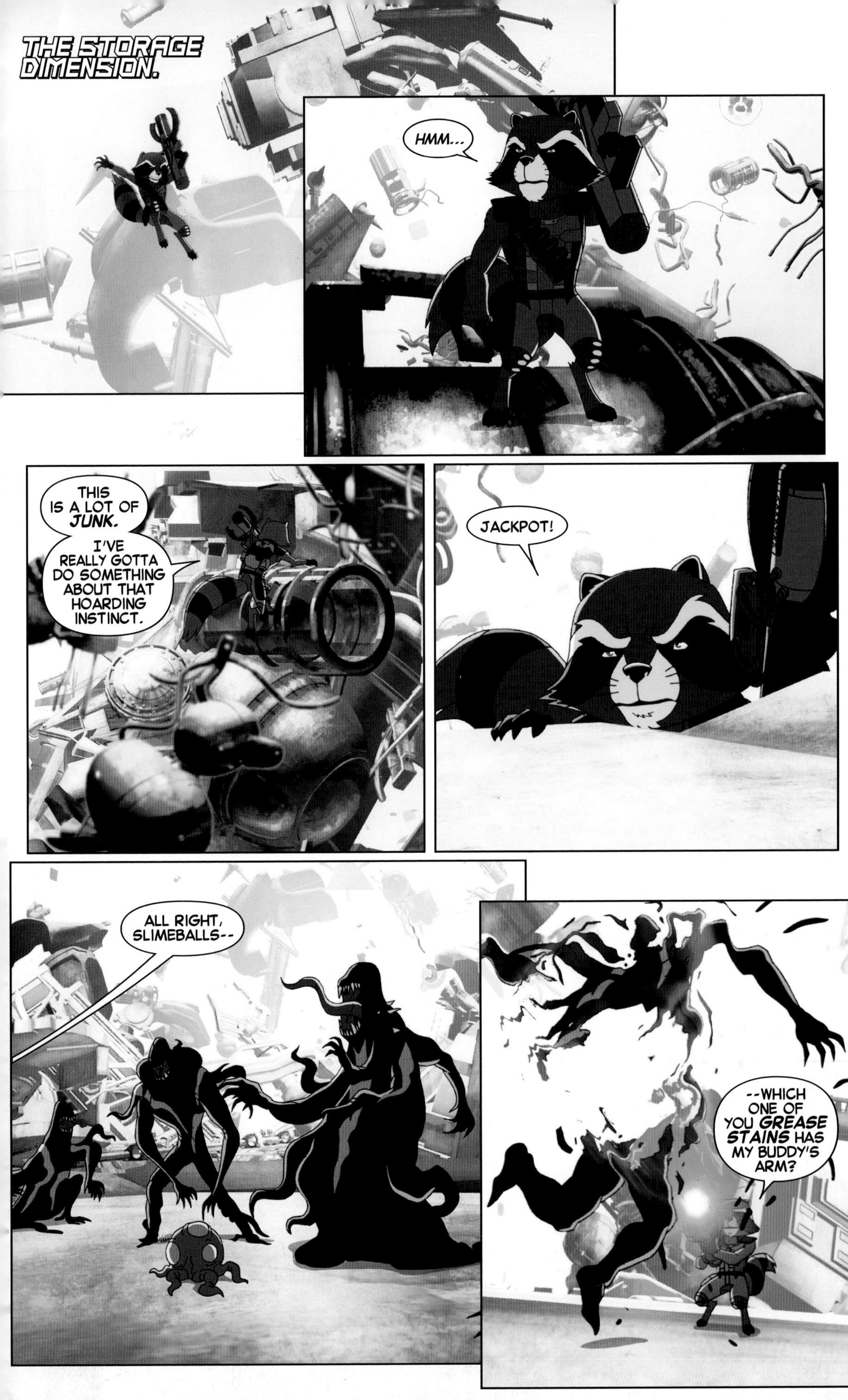
THE STORAGE DIMENSION.
HMM...
THIS IS A LOT OF JUNK.
I'VE REALLY GOTTA DO SOMETHING ABOUT THAT HOARDING INSTINCT.
JACKPOT!
ALL RIGHT, SLIMEBALLS--
--WHICH ONE OF YOU GREASE STAINS HAS MY BUDDY'S ARM?

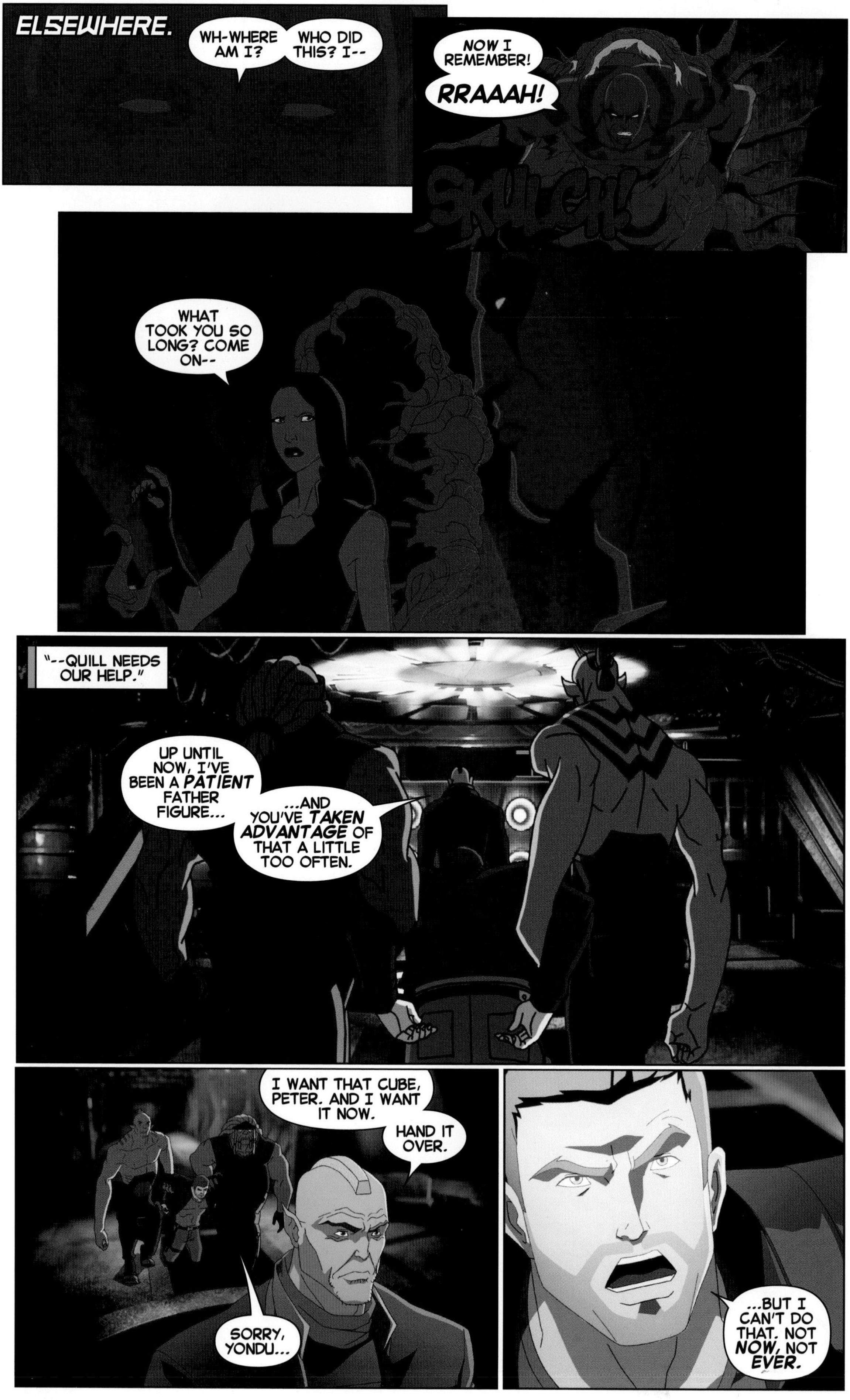
ELSEWHERE.
WH-WHERE AM I?
WHO DID THIS? I--
NOW I REMEMBER!
RRAAAH!
SKLLCH!
WHAT TOOK YOU SO LONG? COME ON--
"--QUILL NEEDS OUR HELP."
UP UNTIL NOW, I'VE BEEN A PATIENT FATHER FIGURE...
...AND YOU'VE TAKEN ADVANTAGE OF THAT A LITTLE TOO OFTEN.
I WANT THAT CUBE, PETER. AND I WANT IT NOW.
HAND IT OVER.
SORRY, YONDU...
...BUT I CAN'T DO THAT. NOT NOW, NOT EVER.

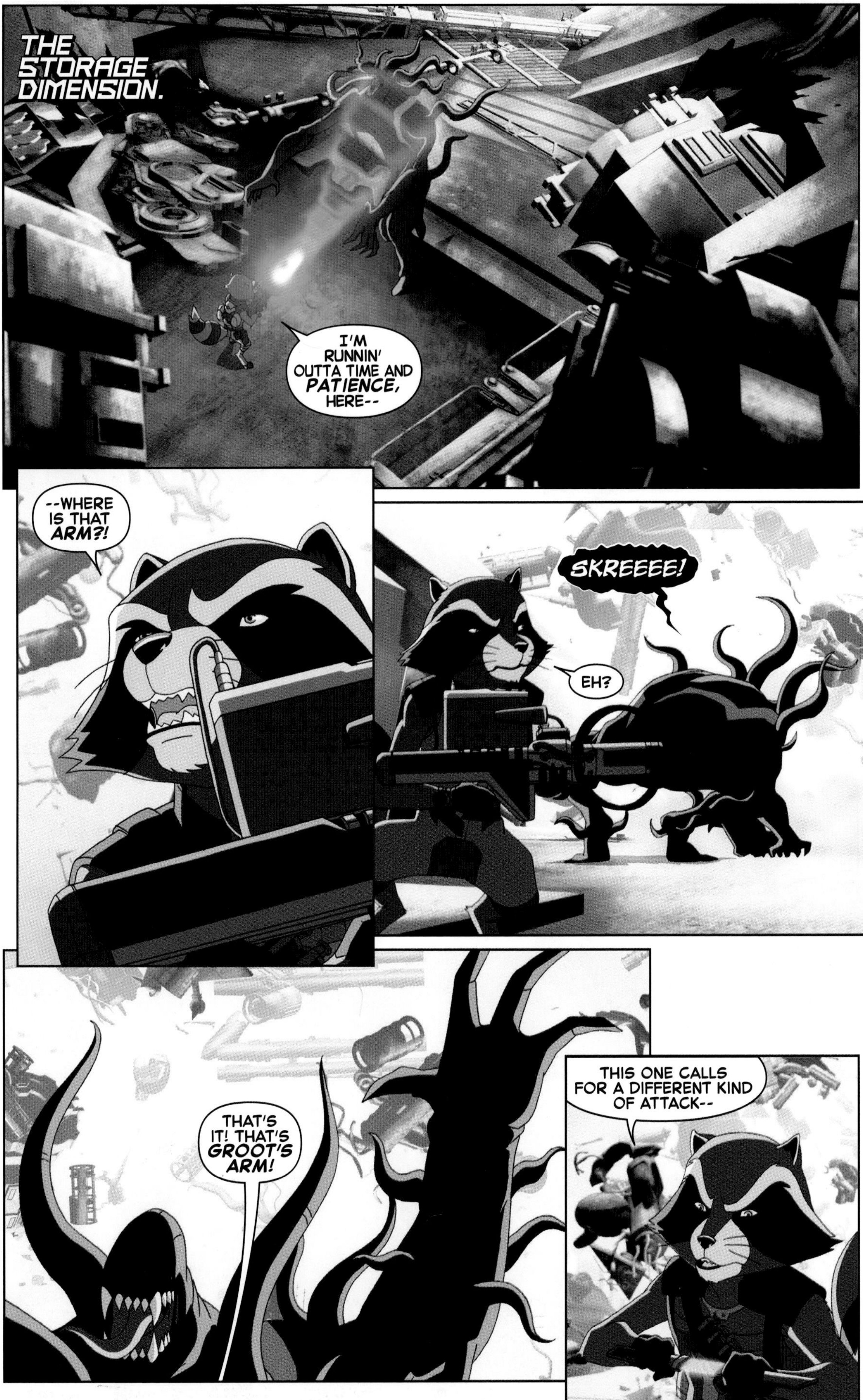
THE STORAGE DIMENSION.
I'M RUNNIN' OUTTA TIME AND PATIENCE, HERE--
--WHERE IS THAT ARM?!
SKREEEE!
EH?
THAT'S IT! THAT'S GROOT'S ARM!
THIS ONE CALLS FOR A DIFFERENT KIND OF ATTACK--

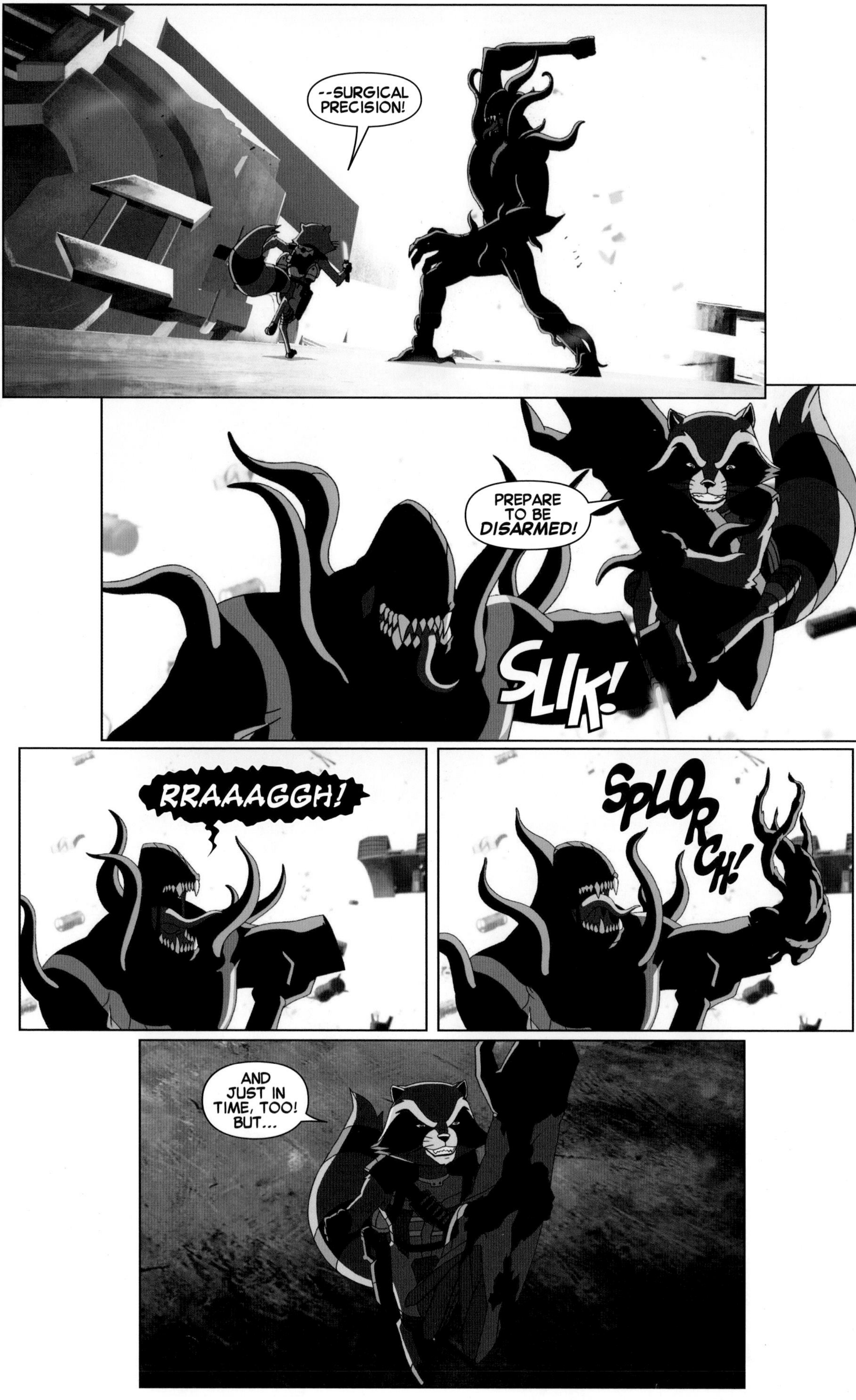
--SURGICAL PRECISION!
PREPARE TO BE DISARMED!
SLIK!
RRAAAGGH!
SPLORCH!
AND JUST IN TIME, TOO! BUT...

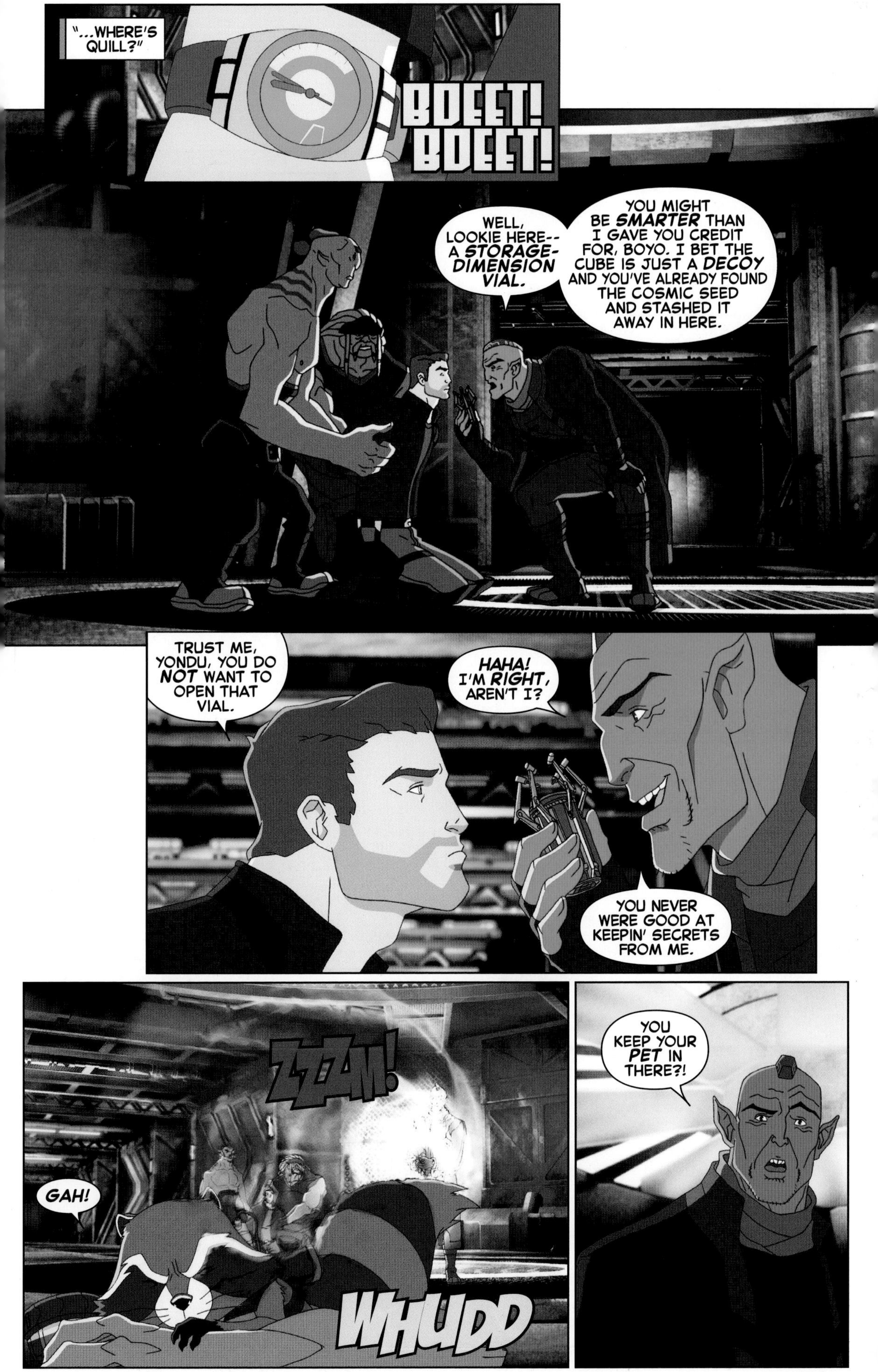
"...WHERE'S QUILL?"
BDEET! BDEET!
WELL, LOOKIE HERE--A STORAGE-DIMENSION VIAL.
YOU MIGHT BE SMARTER THAN I GAVE YOU CREDIT FOR, BOYO. I BET THE CUBE IS JUST A DECOY AND YOU'VE ALREADY FOUND THE COSMIC SEED AND STASHED IT AWAY IN HERE.
TRUST ME, YONDU, YOU DO NOT WANT TO OPEN THAT VIAL.
HAHA! I'M RIGHT, AREN'T I?
YOU NEVER WERE GOOD AT KEEPIN' SECRETS FROM ME.
ZZZM!
GAH!
WHUDD
YOU KEEP YOUR PET IN THERE?!

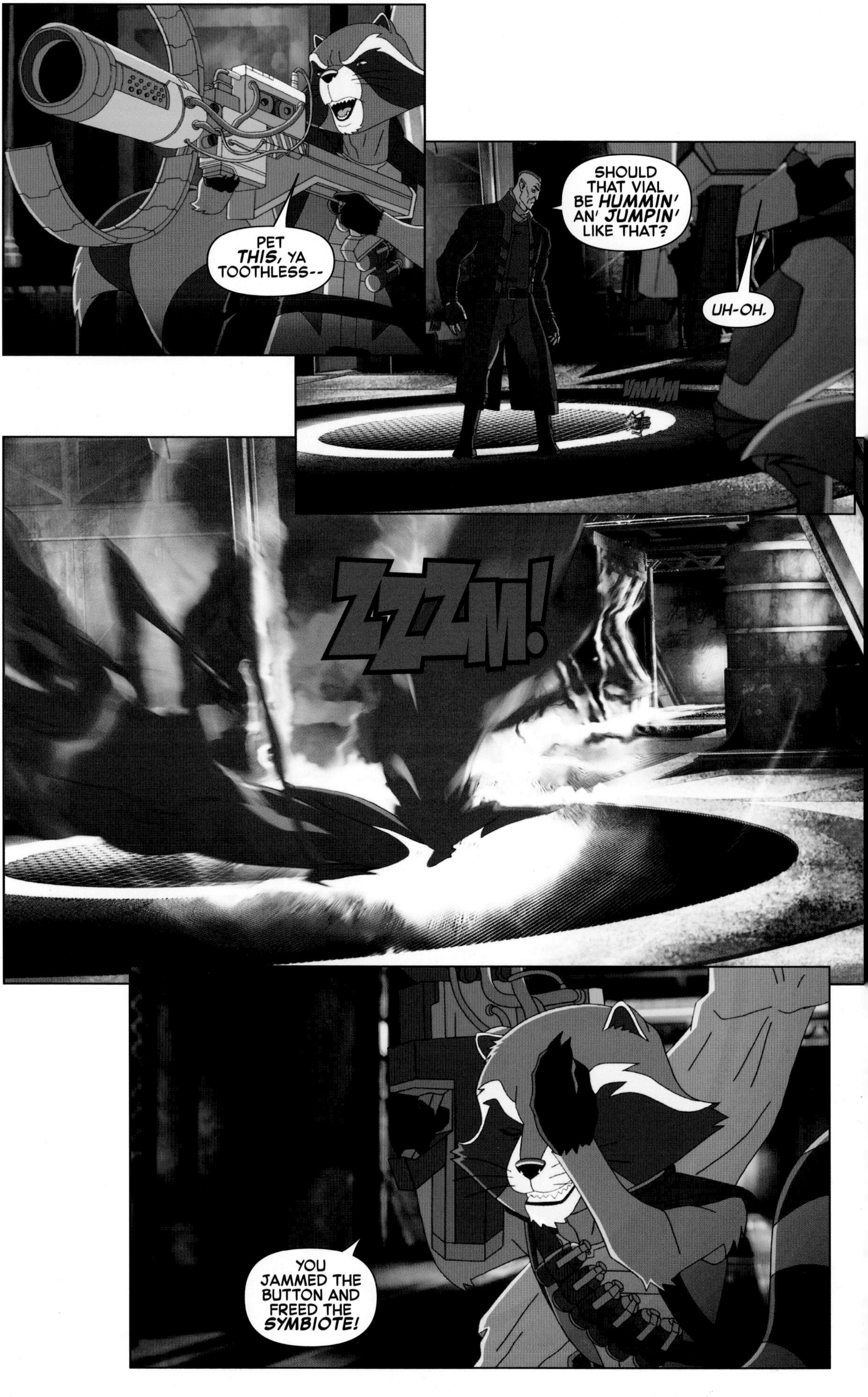
PET THIS, YA TOOTHLESS--
SHOULD THAT VIAL BE HUMMIN' AN' JUMPIN' LIKE THAT?
UH-OH.
ZZZM!
YOU JAMMED THE BUTTON AND FREED THE SYMBIOTE!

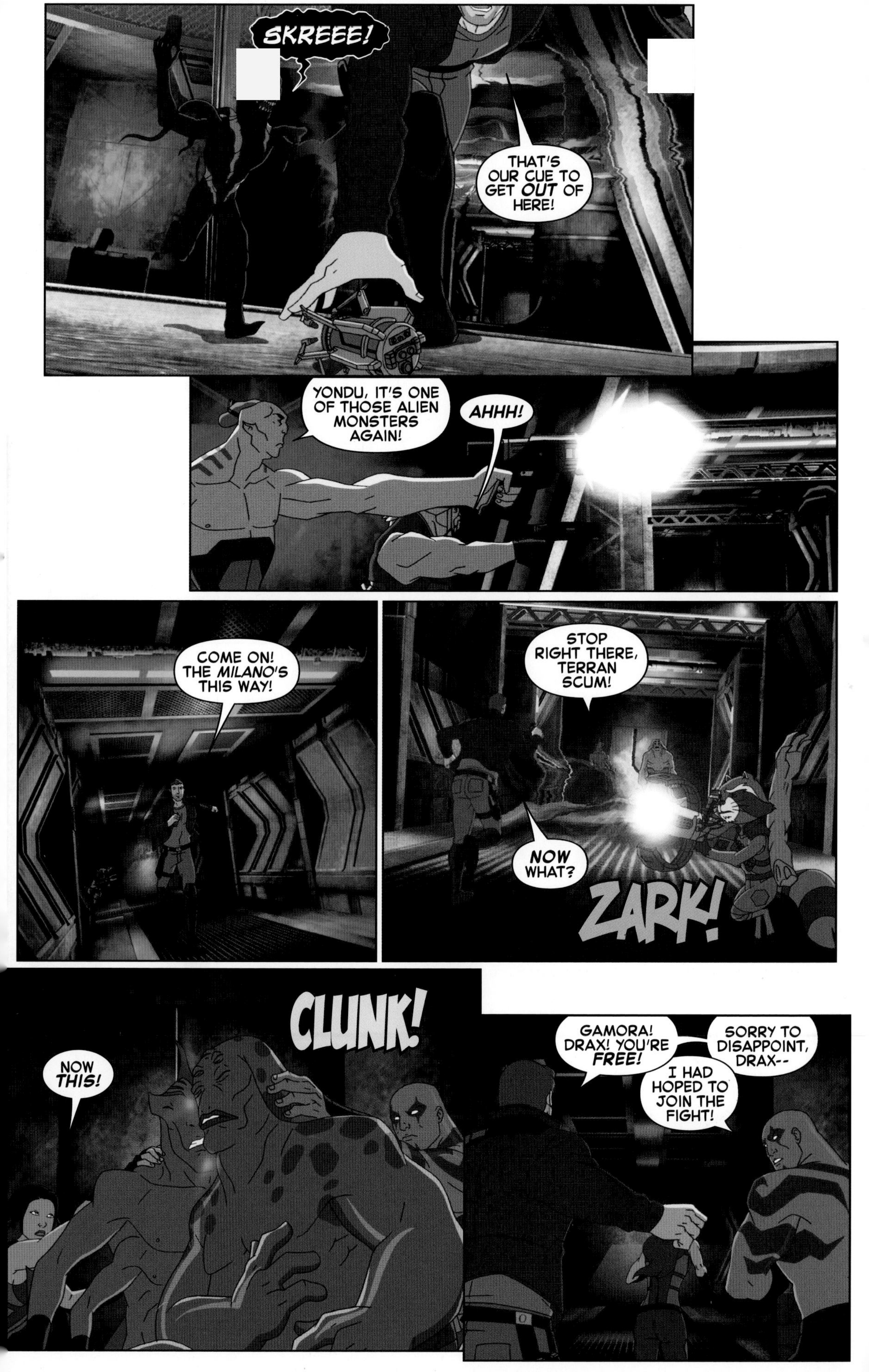
SKREEE!
THAT'S OUR CUE TO GET *OUT* OF HERE!
YONDU, IT'S ONE OF THOSE ALIEN MONSTERS AGAIN!
AHHH!
COME ON! THE *MILANO'S* THIS WAY!
STOP RIGHT THERE, TERRAN SCUM!
NOW WHAT?
ZARK!
CLUNK!
NOW *THIS!*
GAMORA! DRAX! YOU'RE *FREE!*
SORRY TO DISAPPOINT, DRAX--
I HAD HOPED TO JOIN THE FIGHT!

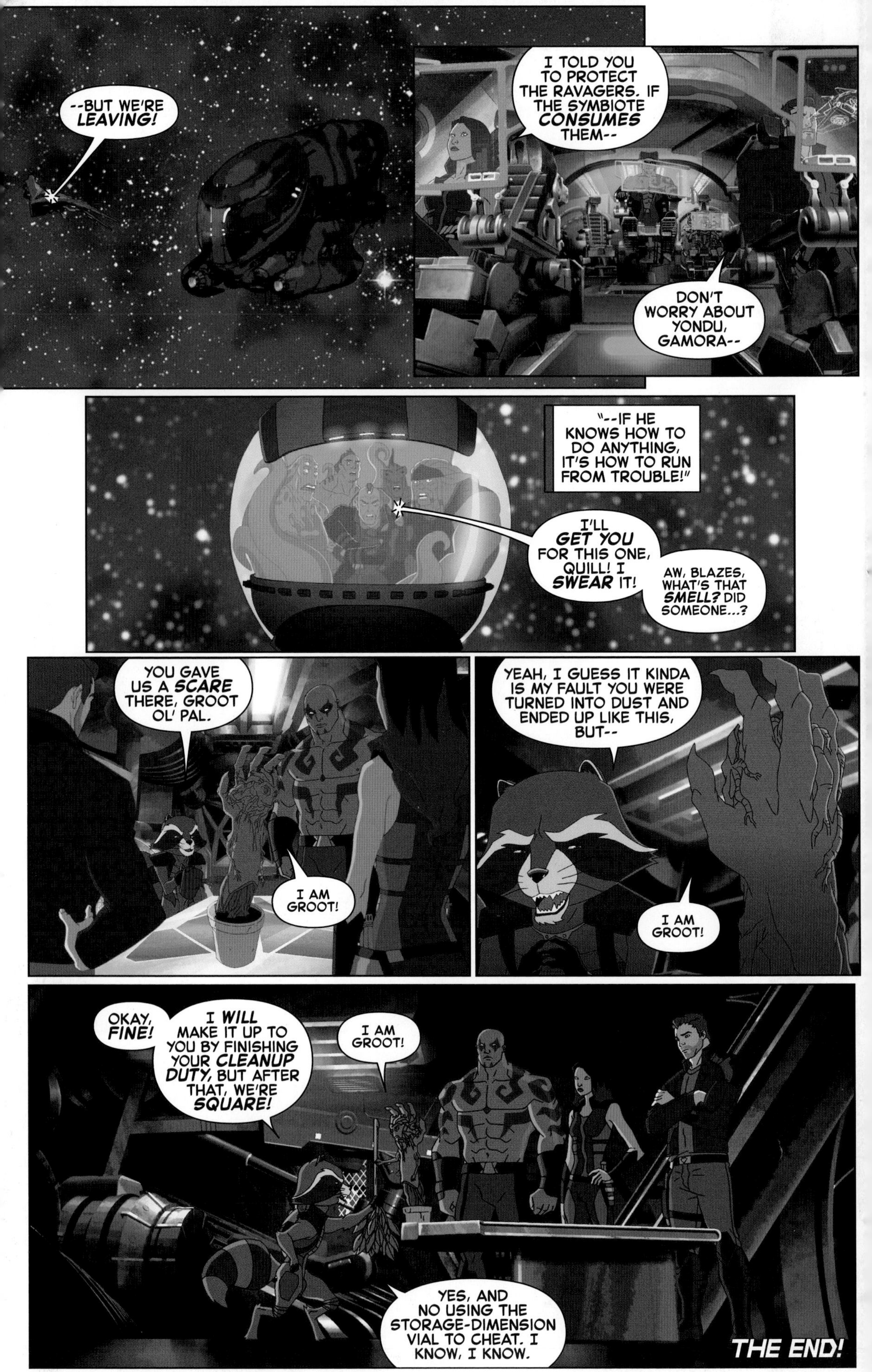
--BUT WE'RE LEAVING!
I TOLD YOU TO PROTECT THE RAVAGERS. IF THE SYMBIOTE CONSUMES THEM--
DON'T WORRY ABOUT YONDU, GAMORA--
"--IF HE KNOWS HOW TO DO ANYTHING, IT'S HOW TO RUN FROM TROUBLE!"
I'LL GET YOU FOR THIS ONE, QUILL! I SWEAR IT!
AW, BLAZES, WHAT'S THAT SMELL? DID SOMEONE...?
YOU GAVE US A SCARE THERE, GROOT OL' PAL.
I AM GROOT!
YEAH, I GUESS IT KINDA IS MY FAULT YOU WERE TURNED INTO DUST AND ENDED UP LIKE THIS, BUT--
I AM GROOT!
OKAY, FINE!
I WILL MAKE IT UP TO YOU BY FINISHING YOUR CLEANUP DUTY, BUT AFTER THAT, WE'RE SQUARE!
I AM GROOT!
YES, AND NO USING THE STORAGE-DIMENSION VIAL TO CHEAT. I KNOW, I KNOW.
THE END!

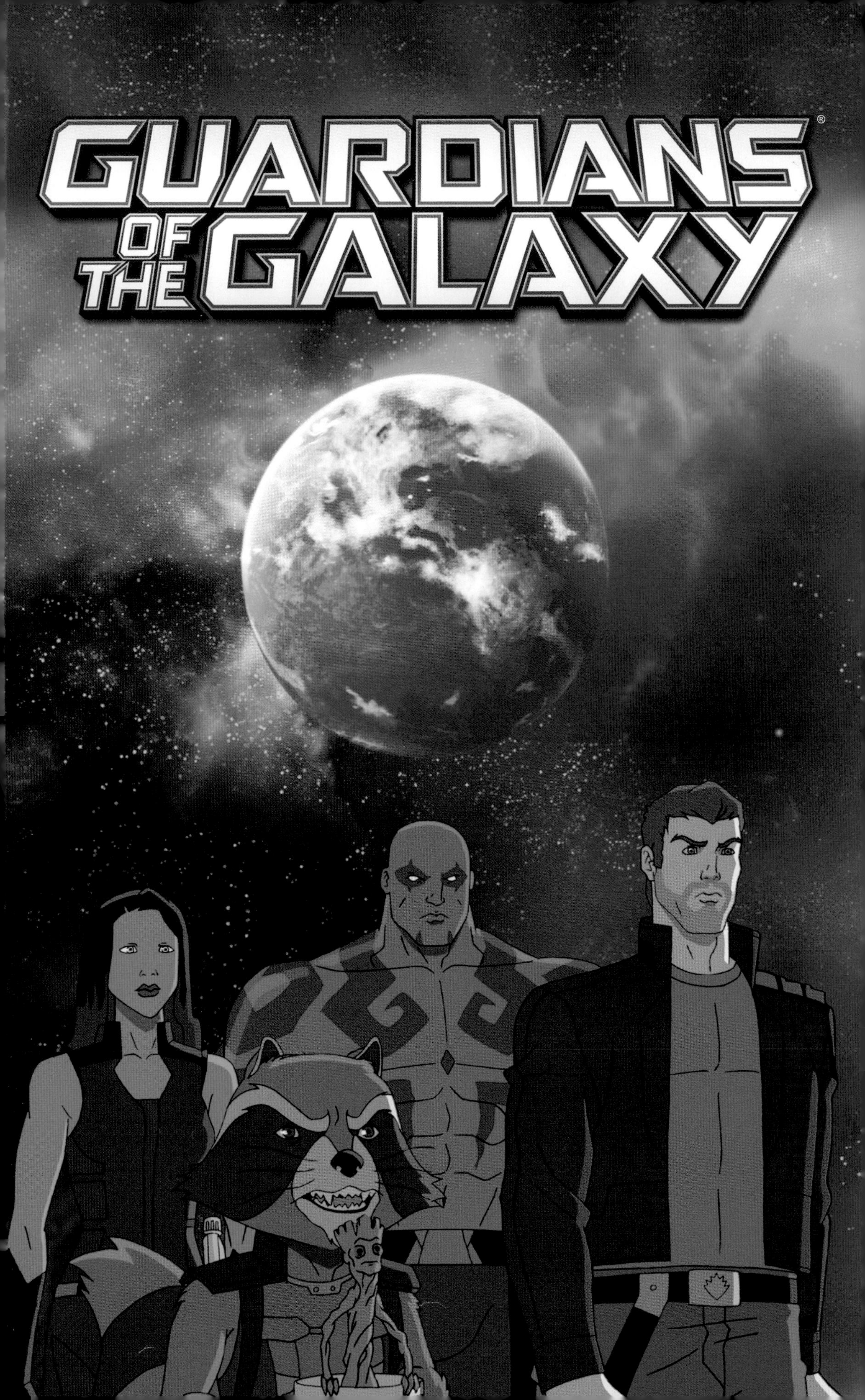
GUARDIANS OF THE GALAXY

GUARDIANS OF THE GALAXY®

COLLECT THEM ALL!

Set of 6 Hardcover Books ISBN: 978-1-5321-4357-1

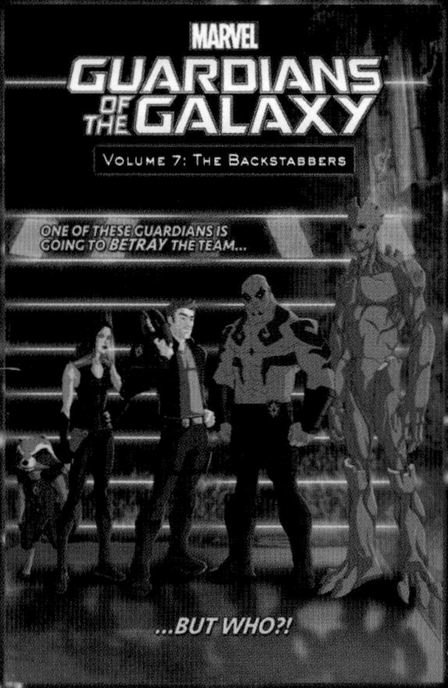

MARVEL
GUARDIANS OF THE GALAXY
Volume 7: The Backstabbers
ONE OF THESE GUARDIANS IS GOING TO BETRAY THE TEAM...
...BUT WHO?!

Hardcover Book ISBN 978-1-5321-4358-8

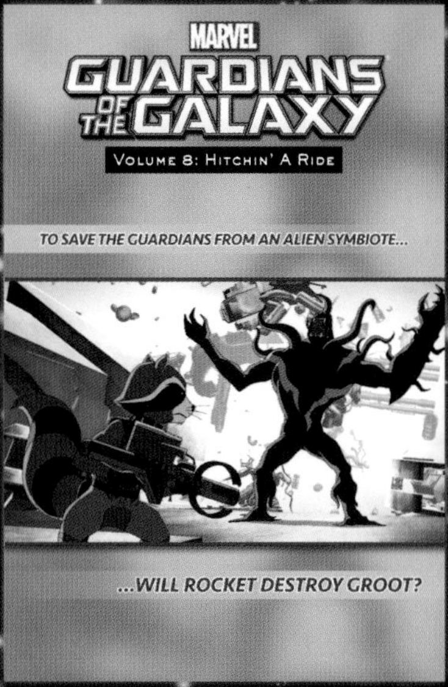

MARVEL
GUARDIANS OF THE GALAXY
Volume 8: Hitchin' A Ride
TO SAVE THE GUARDIANS FROM AN ALIEN SYMBIOTE...
...WILL ROCKET DESTROY GROOT?

Hardcover Book ISBN 978-1-5321-4359-5

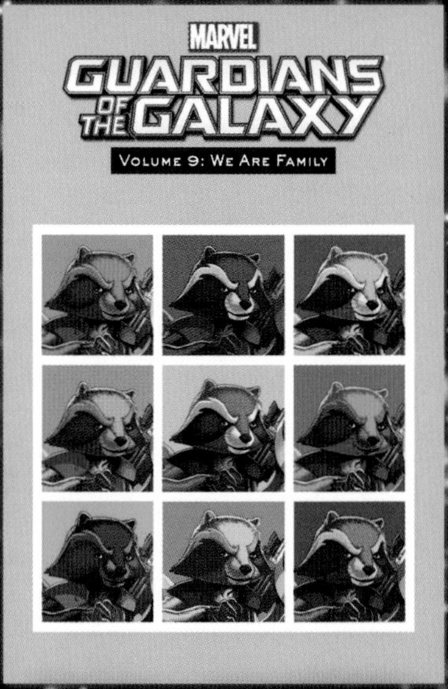

MARVEL
GUARDIANS OF THE GALAXY
Volume 9: We Are Family

Hardcover Book ISBN 978-1-5321-4360-1

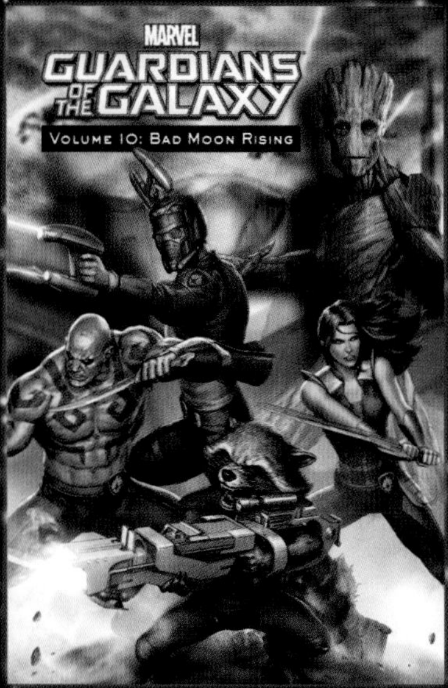

MARVEL
GUARDIANS OF THE GALAXY
Volume 10: Bad Moon Rising

Hardcover Book ISBN 978-1-5321-4361-8

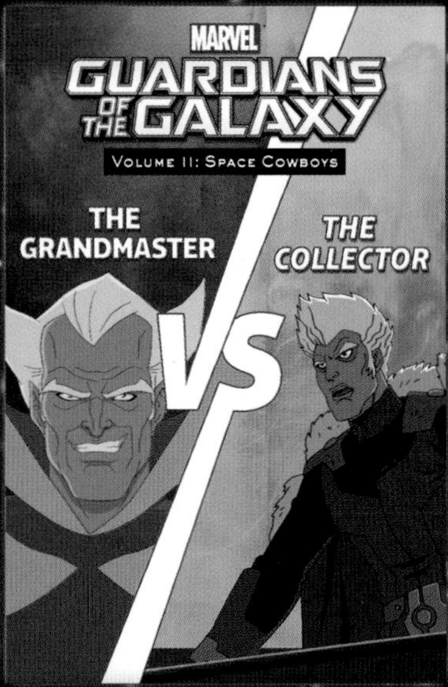

MARVEL
GUARDIANS OF THE GALAXY
Volume 11: Space Cowboys
THE GRANDMASTER
VS
THE COLLECTOR

Hardcover Book ISBN 978-1-5321-4362-5

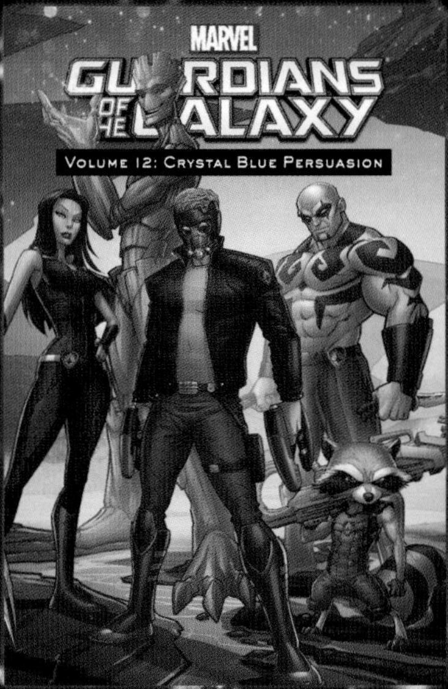

MARVEL
GUARDIANS OF THE GALAXY
Volume 12: Crystal Blue Persuasion

Hardcover Book ISBN 978-1-5321-4363-2